Mel Bay Presents
Classic Bluegrass Solos for *Mandolin*

By Todd Collins

1 2 3 4 5 6 7 8 9 0

© 2007 BY MEL BAY PUBLICATIONS, INC., PACIFIC, MO 63069.
ALL RIGHTS RESERVED. INTERNATIONAL COPYRIGHT SECURED. B.M.I. MADE AND PRINTED IN U.S.A.
No part of this publication may be reproduced in whole or in part, or stored in a retrieval system, or transmitted in any form
or by any means, electronic, mechanical, photocopy, recording, or otherwise, without written permission of the publisher.

Visit us on the Web at www.melbay.com — E-mail us at email@melbay.com

CONTENTS

Introduction • 3
Keys of Tunes • 3
Scales and Positions • 4
Chords and Positions for Tunes • 7
Key for Symbols • 8
A Good Woman's Love • 11
Blue Grass Stomp • 12
Highway of Sorrow • 15
I am a Pilgrim • 16
I'm On My Way to the Old Home • 17
I'm Working on a Building (#1) • 18
I'm Working on a Building (#2) • 20
John Hardy • 22
Letter from My Darling • 24
Lord Protect My Soul • 26
Midnight on the Stormy Deep • 27
Nine Pound Hammer • 28
On and On • 29
On the Old Kentucky Shore • 30
Raw Hide • 32
Sitting Alone in the Moonlight • 34
Uncle Pen • 35
Used to Be • 36
Walk Softly on This Heart of Mine • 37
Walls of Time • 38
White House Blues • 39
With Body and Soul • 42
Discography for Solos • 43
Todd Collins • 45

CREDITS

CLASSIC BLUEGRASS SOLOS was transcribed and written by Todd Collins.

Text edited by Monica J. Smith.

This book is dedicated to the memory of my father "Rip" Collins and grandmother "Nan" Mack.

Special thanks to Mike Marmor for his generosity and a big thanks and hug to Monica for her insight and help.

Photo of Todd Collins by Brenda Ladd – www.brendaladdphoto.com

Please visit my web site at: www.toddcollinsmusic.com

Check out another book by Todd Collins -
Monroe Instrumentals: 25 Bill Monroe Favorites
Published by Mel Bay Publications, Inc.

And his traditional bluegrass CD called "Blue Soul".

INTRODUCTION

Bill Monroe's playing, steeped in spirit and deep with soul, incorporated blues licks, fiddle tunes, jazz syncopation, and burning breakdowns. His fusion of styles created a new genre of music that became known as bluegrass. Characterized by complex vocal arrangements and virtuosic instrumental breaks, bluegrass raised the bar for traditional American string band music. Monroe's unique mandolin voice could float over the band with tremolos, or drive the band with his eighth-note solos and back-beat chop. He had a major influence on mandolinists since his duet days with his brother Charlie in the '30's and his playing continues to have an impact on players today. These diverse kick-offs, turnarounds, and solos will help you to analyze Monroe's ideas and give you a solid foundation for playing traditional bluegrass, the way Bill Monroe played it.

KEYS OF TUNES

KEY: A
I'm On My Way to the Old Home
I'm Working on a Building (#1)
Sitting Alone in the Moonlight
Uncle Pen
Walk Softly on This Heart of Mine
With Body and Soul

KEY: B
I am a Pilgrim
White House Blues

KEY: C
Nine Pound Hammer
Raw Hide
Used to Be
Walls of Time

KEY: D
Blue Grass Stomp

KEY: E
Highway of Sorrow
Midnight on the Stormy Deep

KEY: F
On the Old Kentucky Shore

KEY: G
A Good Woman's Love
I'm Working on a Building (#2)
John Hardy
Letter from My Darling
Lord Protect My Soul
On and On

SCALES AND POSITIONS

The following chord positions, scales, and fingerings are all used with the solo transcriptions.

#1. 2nd inversion (meaning starting with the 5th of the scale) A major scale; starting with an E (pinky) at the 9th fret. The roots of the scale are located at the 7th fret D string and 5th fret E string. The scale continues past the root on the 5th fret on the E string up to the 3rd of the scale, C# (pinky).

*The same position, scale, and fingering is applied to #3 C, #5 G, and #9 B.

#2. C major scale root position starting with third finger at the 5th fret of the G string.

#3. 2nd inversion C major scale. Same fingering as #1 except start at the 12th fret of the G string with the pinky.

#4. G major scale starting with an open G.

#5. 2nd inversion G major scale. Same fingering as #1 except start two frets lower on the G string.

#6. E major scale root position starting with first finger on second fret of the D string, ending with the pinky at the 7th fret of the A string.

#7. E major scale root position starting with the third finger at the 9th fret of the G string. SHIFT = first finger moves from the 6th fret of the A string up to the 7th fret of the A string. The reverse happens in the descending scale.

#8. F major scale root position. Same fingering as #6 except start at the 3rd fret of the D string.

#9. 2nd inversion B major scale. Same fingering as #1 except start at the 11th fret of the G string.

#10. D major scale root position. Same fingering as #7 except start at the 7th fret of the G string.

SCALES AND POSITIONS

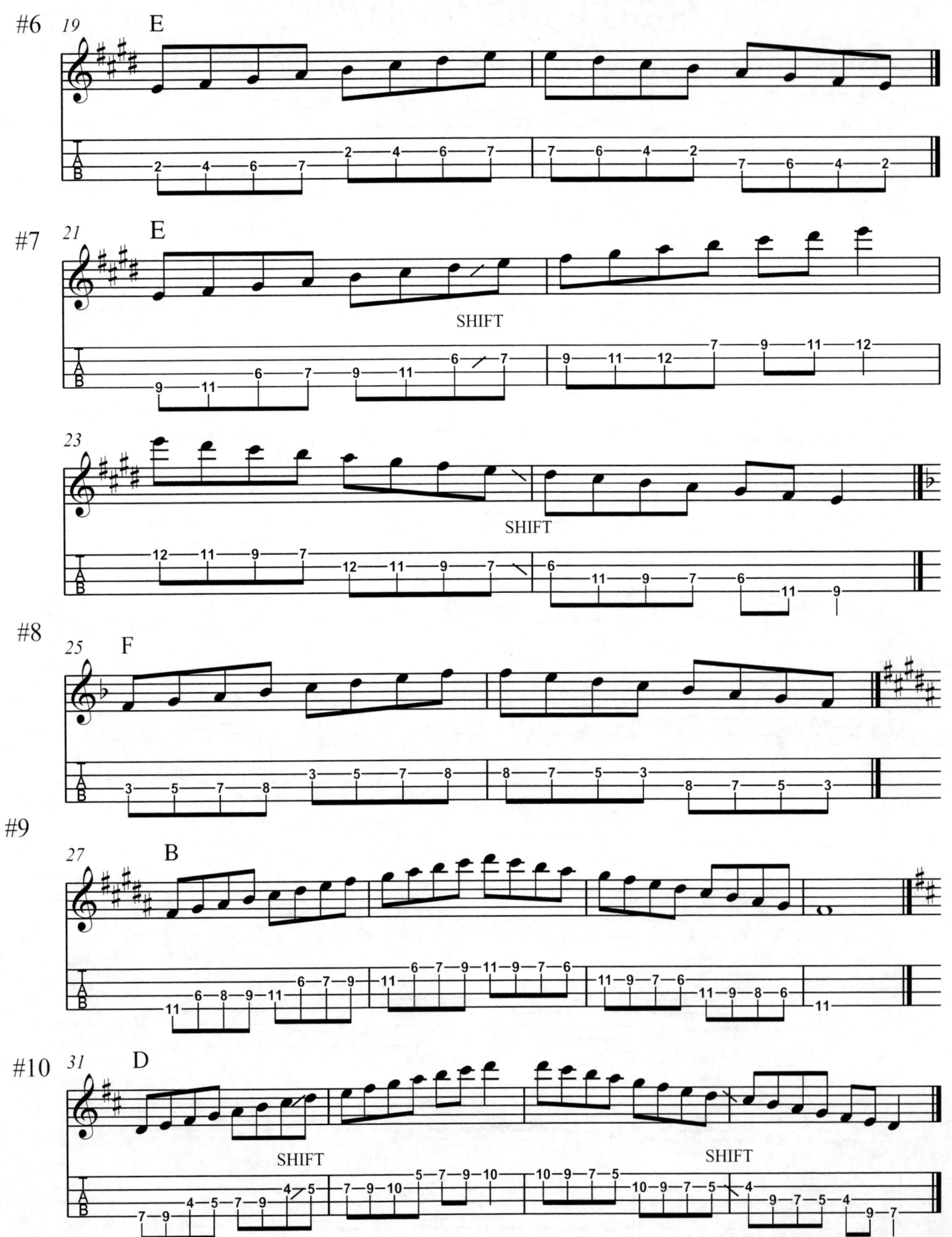

CHORDS AND POSITIONS FOR TUNES

The following are chords and their positions to use for the chord progressions of the transcribed songs.

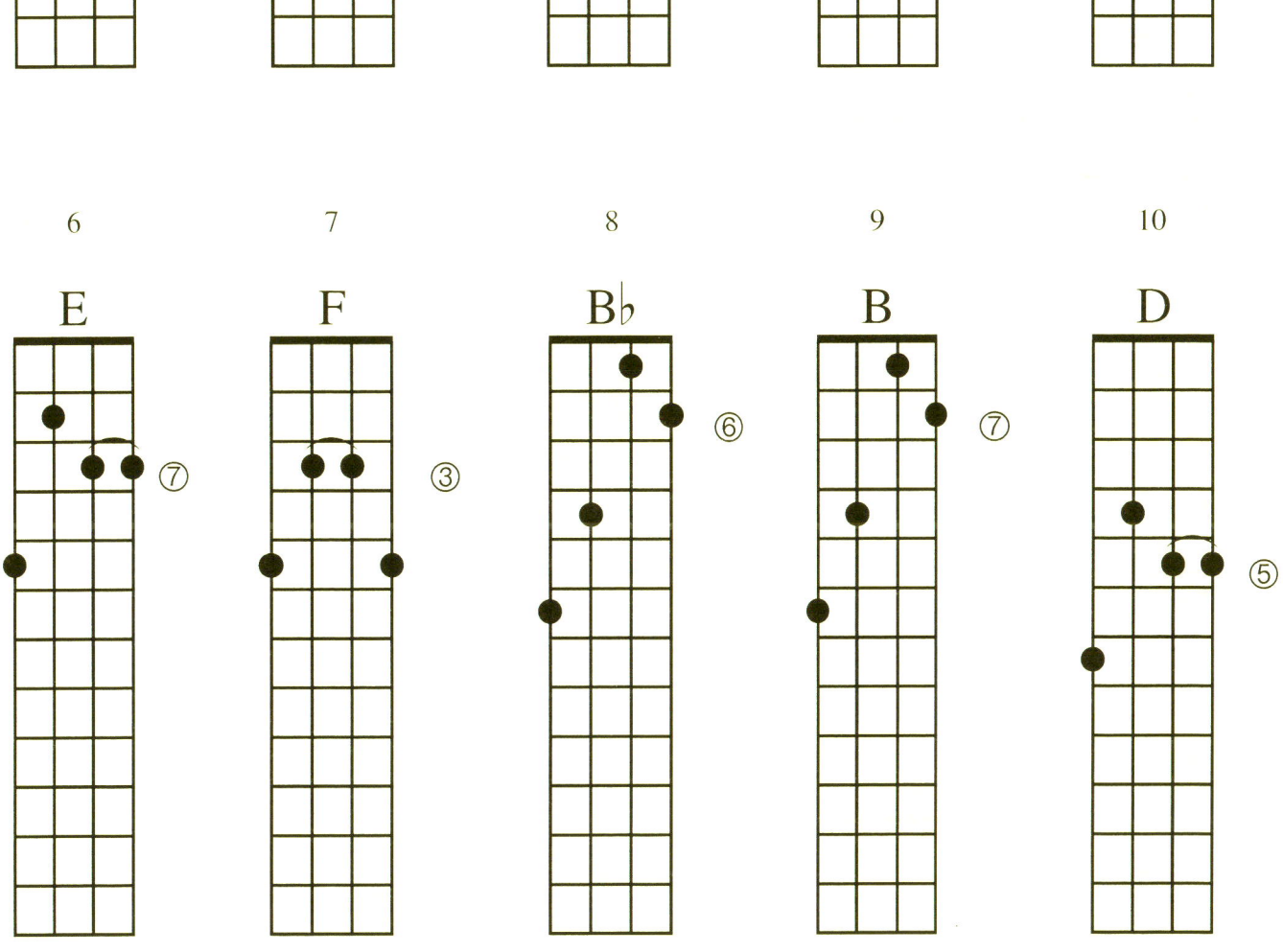

KEY FOR SYMBOLS

#1 Grace note = fast slide into connecting note.

#2 HO = Hammer-On, PO = Pull-Off

#3 & #4 Slide into note.

#5 Short sounding note.

#6 Downstroke

#7 Indeterminate slide from note.

#8 Muted note

#9 Harmonic

#10 Tremelo

This page has been left blank to avoid awkward page turns.

A GOOD WOMAN'S LOVE

This song is a waltz with a 6/8 or triplet feel to it. Monroe stays close to the melody but adds some bluesy phrasing by sliding the minor third (B♭) to the major third (B) at several points.
Recorded in Nashville, May 14, 1957.

by Cy Coben

© 1956 Delmore Music Company. All Rights Reserved. Used by Permission.

BLUE GRASS STOMP

"Blue Grass Stomp" is a 12-bar blues in the key of D. This is the only solo transcribed here in D and Monroe has some great ideas for playing in the upper position in that key. In the first solo, Monroe uses a beautiful tremelo to slide from the 5th and 7th frets up to the 9th and 12th frets and back down again. He continues this tremelo idea throughout the rest of the form in the first half of the solo.

In the second solo, Monroe uses more open strings throughout the solo similar to the head of the tune. In the first several bars, Monroe plays a dissonant G♯ (flat 5th) and alternates between the A and G♯. He resolves each phrase on the tonic preceded with a bluesy slide into the major third. Very cool!
Recorded in Nashville, October 22, 1949.

© 1950 (Renewed) UNICHAPPELL MUSIC INC. All Rights Reserved. Used by Permission.

HIGHWAY OF SORROW

Monroe gives us a lesson here for playing in the upper register of the mandolin in the key of E. Recorded in Nashville, January 27, 1964.

by Bill Monroe and Pete Pyle

I AM A PILGRIM

"I am a Pilgrim" is a Merle Travis classic recording that provides some valuable exercises for playing turnarounds in the key of B.
Recorded in Nashville, March 20, 1958.

Traditional

I'M ON MY WAY TO THE OLD HOME

This tune was written after a visit to his boyhood home in Rosine, Kentucky. Here the recording sounds a half-step high. It may sound like they are in B♭, but they are really playing in the key of A. The open strings on the mandolin solo are what give the key away. No electronic tuners at this time and I have never heard of Monroe using a capo on the mandolin. This is an example of Monroe playing the melody with a constant alternating picking in the right hand.

Recorded in Nashville, February 3, 1950.

by Bill Monroe

© 1950 (Renewed) UNICHAPPELL MUSIC INC. All Rights Reserved. Used by Permission.

I'M WORKING ON A BUILDING (#1)

A gospel tune that kicks off with an excellent turnaround in A. Monroe uses a hammer-on to the C natural (3rd fret A string), a "blues" note, creating some tension with a minor third against a major chord. This is a common practice with playing the blues. On the second solo Monroe plays in a closed position with lots of work for the pinky. A solo filled with syncopation.
Recorded in Nashville, January 25, 1954.

Traditional

I'M WORKING ON A BUILDING (#2)

Another version of "I'm Working on a Building" in the key of G that is from a live recording in 1956. I selected this solo as an excellent example of Monroe's use of syncopation and blues notes. He is quoted as saying, "You know there's holiness singing in my music, bluegrass music." And a lot of soul too, Mr. Monroe! Recorded at New River Ranch, Rising Sun, Maryland, May 13, 1956.

Traditional

This page has been left blank to avoid awkward page turns.

JOHN HARDY

Here is a brisk instrumental version of "John Hardy", the desperate little man. Monroe plays a nice melodic solo with fine use of double stops.
Recorded in Nashville, December 4, 1961.

Traditional

LETTER FROM MY DARLING

Another beautiful bluesy solo with a dotted 8th note or swing feel to it. Notice the continuous driving downstrokes in the beginning of his solo, a technique Monroe liked to use on some medium tempo tunes. This is a style very similar to what Chuck Berry came up with for rock and roll guitar. Chuck listened to country music and Monroe in particular. Could Monroe have influenced Chuck's playing?
Recorded in Nashville, January 20, 1951.

by Bill Monroe

© 1951 (Renewed) UNICHAPPELL MUSIC INC. All Rights Reserved. Used by Permission.

LORD PROTECT MY SOUL

Here are some classic Monroe turnarounds in G with a signature ending lick in bars 3, 4, and 5. Note the downstroke in the beginning of the second turnaround flowing right into the famous triplet lick. Recorded in Nashville, October 15, 1950.

by Bill Monroe

© 1951 (Renewed) UNICHAPPELL MUSIC INC. All Rights Reserved. Used by Permission.

MIDNIGHT ON THE STORMY DEEP

The only duet Peter Rowan and Bill Monroe ever recorded in the studio. Here, Monroe plays a nice turnaround in E. Note how he ends the phrase at the 6th and 7th frets – the root and 3rd of the chord. For the solo, Monroe stays close to the melody. At bars 9 and 10 he uses a fast hammer-on to the G, a "blues" note (lowered 7th of the A major chord). A very effective lick. Recorded in Nashville, December 16-17, 1966.

Traditional

NINE POUND HAMMER

In "Nine Pound Hammer" Monroe again follows the chord progressions closely with the use of double-stops in the first half of the solo. In the second bar he plays an E and B♭, which is the 3rd and lowered 7th of the C major chord. He opens the solo with the constant downstroke technique. Some fine use of syncopation throughout.
Recorded in Nashville, November 10, 1961.

Traditional

ON AND ON

This autobiographical "true" tune is from one of my favorite (and my first) Monroe LP's, *The High, Lonesome Sound of Bill Monroe and His Blue Grass Boys*. Monroe starts off "On and On" with a tremelo into the signature G major pentatonic arpeggiated lick in the second bar, and finishes bars 14, 15, and 16 with his classic blues ending.
Recorded in Nashville, January 25, 1954.

by Bill Monroe

© 1956 (Renewed) UNICHAPPELL MUSIC INC. All Rights Reserved. Used by Permission.

ON THE OLD KENTUCKY SHORE

Also from *The High, Lonesome Sound...* LP, this tune is a study in F, an unusual key for Monroe. Even though this is a waltz, it is subdivided into triplets for each beat, and therefore it is in 9/8 time. Monroe slips around with his tremelo in both the intro and solo.
Recorded in Nashville, January 20, 1951.

by Bill Monroe

© 1951 (Renewed) UNICHAPPELL MUSIC INC. All Rights Reserved. Used by Permission.

This page has been left blank to avoid awkward page turns.

RAW HIDE

Named after an old Western film, "Raw Hide" is a Monroe tour de force tune and one every bluegrass mandolinist needs to know. The "A" section up-the-neck break showcases his virtuosity. Recorded in Nashville, January 20, 1951.

by Bill Monroe

© 1951 (Renewed) UNICHAPPELL MUSIC INC. All Rights Reserved. Used by Permission.

SITTING ALONE IN THE MOONLIGHT

For those of you playing along I know what you are wondering: Dude, what's the deal here? Isn't this tune in B♭? Well, yes and no. On the recording it is in B♭, but analysis of Monroe's solo clearly reveals that he is using open strings. Therefore, he must have been tuned a half-step too high, so that an open A string sounds like a B♭. "Sitting Alone" is another waltz with a 9/8 feel. Note the lovely progression where he moves from A to A♭ and back up.

Recorded in Nashville, January 19, 1954.

by Bill Monroe

© 1957 (Renewed) UNICHAPPELL MUSIC INC. All Rights Reserved. Used by Permission.

UNCLE PEN

"Uncle Pen" is named after Monroe's uncle, Pendleton Vandiver, who taught him so much about fiddling. Although the piece is more of a fiddle tune, Monroe plays interesting solos over the "B" section. Recorded in Nashville, October 15, 1950.

by Bill Monroe

© 1951 (Renewed) UNICHAPPELL MUSIC INC. All Rights Reserved. Used by Permission.

USED TO BE

Another fine study in the key of C with a combination of ideas – tremeloed double-stops, blues notes, and syncopation.
Recorded in Nashville, September 16, 1955.

by Bill Monroe

© UNICHAPPELL MUSIC, INC. All Rights Reserved. Used by Permission.

WALK SOFTLY ON THIS HEART OF MINE

Here is a beautifully constructed solo in the key of A. The phrase starting at bar 5 and ending on the downbeat of bar 8 is classic Monroe in a closed A position.
Recorded in Mt. Juliet, TN, October 28, 1969.

by Bill Monroe and Jake Landers

© 1977 (Renewed) Bill Monroe Music/BMI (admin. by ICG) All Rights Reserved. Used by Permission.

WALLS OF TIME

"Walls of Time" was written by Monroe and Peter Rowan and is one of my all-time favorite songs. The solo is a masterpiece of melodic construction. Monroe kicks it off right onto the IV chord (F) in the intro. The solo starts off with 16th note pick-ups into a tremeloed tonic note. At the end of the first bar is a device Monroe uses in the key of C. Playing an E♭ at the 6th fret of the A string with an open E string creating a dissonant minor second interval. He repeats this in bar 9. Students need to take note of how to stay close to the melody of a song. Recorded in Nashville, November 14, 1968.

by Bill Monroe and Peter Rowan

© 1973 (Renewed 2001) Bill Monroe Music/BMI (admin. by ICG) All Rights Reserved. Used by Permission.

WHITE HOUSE BLUES

Here are four burning solos by Monroe. Notice his use of open strings even though he is playing up-the-neck. Lots of great ideas in these solos but one of my favorite licks is in the second solo. The solo starts with a double-stop at the 7th and 9th frets in a syncopated pattern. Then in the third measure Monroe sticks a finger down on the 10th fret of the E string, which is the lowered 3rd (blues note) and plays it in a staccato, on-the-beat, driving rhythm. "…anything I play couldn't sound nothing but bluegrass" Monroe said, and this is the epitome of hard driving bluegrass.
Recorded in Nashville, January 25, 1954.

by Wilbur Jones

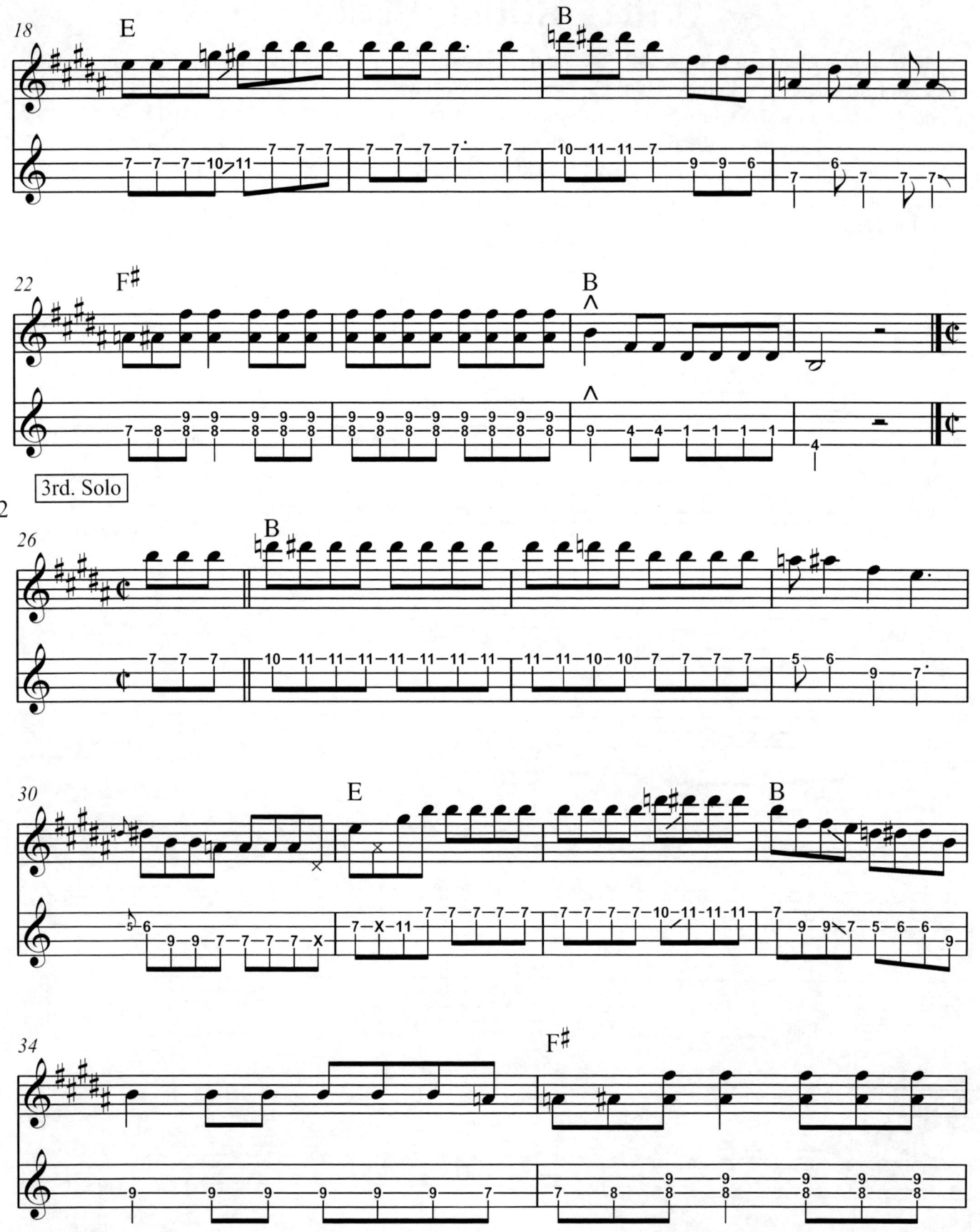

WITH BODY AND SOUL

Monroe plays a simple solo that stays close to the melody but with lots of soul. The final phrase starting at bar 6 to the end is a classic closed position move.
Recorded in Nashville, April 29, 1969.

by Virginia Stauffer

© 1975 (Renewed) Bill Monroe Music/BMI (admin. by ICG) All Rights Reserved. Used by Permission.

DISCOGRAPHY FOR SOLOS

CD's:

Bill Monroe - Blue Grass 1950 - 1958 Bear Family Records - Four CD set:
A Good Woman's Love
I am a Pilgrim
I'm On My Way to the Old Home
I'm Working on a Building (#1)
Letter from My Darling
Lord Protect My Soul
On and On
On the Old Kentucky Shore
Raw Hide
Sitting Alone in the Moonlight
Uncle Pen
Used to Be
White House Blues

Bill Monroe -Blue Grass 1959- 1969 Bear Family Records - Four CD set:
Highway of Sorrow
John Hardy
Midnight on the Stormy Deep
Nine Pound Hammer
Walk Softly on This Heart of Mine
Walls of Time
With Body and Soul

The Music of Bill Monroe from 1936 to 1994 MCA Four CD set:
I'm On My Way to the Old Home
Lord Protect My Soul
Midnight on the Stormy Deep
Nine Pound Hammer
On and On
Raw Hide
Sitting Alone in the Moonlight
Uncle Pen
Used to Be
Walk Softly on This Heart of Mine
Walls of Time
White House Blues
With Body and Soul

The Essential Bill Monroe and His Blue Grass Boys 1945 -1949
Columbia Legacy C2K 52478 -Two CD set
Blue Grass Stomp

Bill Monroe and the Bluegrass Boys: Live Recordings 1956 -1969
Off the Record volume 1
Smithsonian Folkways SF CD 40063
I'm Working on a Building (#2)

LP's:

The High Lonesome Sound of Bill Monroe and his Blue Grass Boys
Decca DL7 4780, MCA 110
Highway of Sorrow
Letter from My Darling
On and On
On the Old Kentucky Shore
White House Blues

Blue Grass Ramble
Decca DL7 4266, MCA 88
John Hardy
Nine Pound Hammer

Bluegrass Instrumentals
Decca DL7 4601, MCA 104
Raw Hide

The Best of Bill Monroe
MCA2 – 4090
Two LP set
Highway of Sorrow
Uncle Pen

Knee Deep in Blue Grass
Decca DL 8731
A Good Woman's Love

I Saw the Light
Decca DL 8769
I am a Pilgrim

Bluegrass Time
Decca DL7 4896
Midnight on the Stormy Deep

Sings Bluegrass, Body and Soul
MCA 2251
Walk Softly on this Heart of Mine
With Body and Soul

A Voice from on High
Decca DL7 5135
Lord Protect My Soul
I'm Working on a Building (#1)

TODD COLLINS

Todd Collins performs mainly in the northeastern United States, with forays as far as New Mexico, Maine, Scotland, and England. He performs in a variety of settings ranging from traditional and progressive bluegrass to swing, contemporary jazz, blues, rock, and classical. He has performed with some of the most gifted acoustic musicians on the planet, including legendary fiddlers Vassar Clements and Kenny Kosek, banjo guru Bill Keith, Peter Rowan, and Butch Baldassari's Nashville Mandolin Trio. Todd collaborated with former David Grisman arranger/guitarist John Carlini to form an eclectic acoustic band, Over the Edge. They covered the gamut of musical styles by fusing together traditional bluegrass with jazz, classical, and world music. His current bluegrass recording, "Blue Soul" is getting national attention and airplay across America.

Collins' recording credits include film and television, along with guesting on numerous CD's. He played mandolin for the Disney film soundtrack "Tom and Huck" and a Polaroid commercial. Collins is also a producer who is in demand, with recordings by Over the Edge, The Lost Ramblers, banjoist Terry McGill, and singer/songwriter Tom Nieman.

Todd is an associate professor and coordinator of the Music Technology program at County College of Morris (CCM) located in Randolph, New Jersey. At CCM he has assembled and conducted numerous workshops, seminars, and concerts including the annual event, "A Day of Bluegrass". He also gives workshops for guitar and mandolin in the States and abroad. Todd was the mandolin instructor for the "Bluegrass Masters Workshops" at the popular Big Apple Bluegrass Festival in New York City. His first book of Bill Monroe transcriptions titled "Monroe Instrumentals", is published by Mel Bay Publications, Inc.

Collins has been commissioned to compose works for modern dance companies in the New York/New Jersey area, including Beyond Dance, Inc., the Montclair State University Dance Department, and the County College of Morris Dance Department.

Todd Collins earned a Master of Music in Jazz Studies from Rutgers University and a Bachelor of Music from Montclair State University.

toddcollins@sprintmail.com
www.toddcollinsmusic.com